SPARKLE TO THE SEASON

HELEN JULIET

For everyone who read Glitter on the Garland. You made dreams come true.

TWAS THE NIGHT BEFORE CHRISTMAS

"ARE YOU SURE?" AEDAN GALLAGHER SAID. "COULD YOU check? I really need a dozen in ice blue."

The sales assistant blinked slowly at him. "It's Christmas Eve. Most people have had their decorations up for weeks."

"Ah, well, I'm not most people," said Aedan with a laugh.

The guy stared blankly back at him.

Aedan cleared his throat as people jostled around him. He wasn't going to be intimidated. "You see," he continued in a cheery tone, "they really are beautiful. But I don't know if three will make enough of an impact on the tree."

The sales assistant looked like he was in his mid-twenties, the same as Aedan. Although he was wearing a cheery Santa hat, his stony expression suggested he was a hundred percent done with the festive season, not to mention the heaving throng of people currently bustling through the large shop.

Aedan took comfort from the fact he wasn't the only poor sap stuck out on Oxford Street on December 24th, desperately trying to get everything sorted for the big day tomorrow. Ordinarily, he avoided Britain's busiest high street like the plague. It was always jam packed with slow moving tourists and utterly impractical for normal shopping needs.

But Aedan and his boyfriend Matt had both been so busy with work and getting their new flat redecorated, there had been little time left to get themselves into the Christmas spirit. Luckily, Aedan had finished work at lunchtime that day. His manager had insisted everyone deserved a trip down the pub, but Aedan sadly declined. This was his last chance to get presents, decorations, wrapping paper and anything else he'd not been able to pick up during the rest of December.

Oxford Street was the closest set of shops to his office, and, in theory, had everything he could need. But even on Christmas Eve, it seemed there was only so many miracles to go around.

Normally, he had all these things planned since halfway through November. Christmas was his favourite holiday. The perfect chance to see as many friends as possible and legitimately have cheese and wine for dinner as much as you liked. But it had been such a busy year, his time for preparations had vanished faster than the chocolate from an advent calendar.

Matt was terrible. He'd already gone through three calendars since the start of the month, always giving in to the hidden chocolates before the days they were supposed to be eaten. Thinking of his adorable guilty face when Aedan discovered him each time made him calm down. Once Aedan got through this dreadful shopping trip, Matt would be home not long after and they could start their holiday together.

He did his best to smile at the sales assistant. "Is there not any stock out back?" Aedan was tired; he could hear his Irish accent getting stronger. "You see, I've got this whole Arendelle, ice palace vision. These hanging crystals are just perfect, but I couldn't see any more on the shelf."

The guy sucked his teeth, eyes narrowing. "I'm sorry, *sir,*" he said. His mocking tone sent an immediate shiver down Aedan's spine. He looked Aedan up and down; from his sparkly, Kohl lined eyes, down past the rainbow broach pinned to the coat fitted perfectly to his slim frame, along very skinny jeans to his perfectly shined shoes. Aedan jutted his chin out defiantly, even though he felt uncomfortable. "But like I already explained," the guy sneered, "it's Christmas Eve, and this is the final stock clearance. Everything will be reduced on Boxing Day, then chucked on New Year's Day." He flicked an eyebrow. "If you wanted to make a *fairy* castle, perhaps you should have started sooner."

Without another word, he slouched off into the depths of the department store, scowling at anyone else who dared come near him.

Aedan swallowed. His feet were killing him and he was stressed, worrying how he was going to get everything sorted, even with the shops being open until late. Normally, he would brush off shitty homophobia like that without a second thought. But he didn't have the energy to laugh at the guy. Instead, he bit his lip and readjusted perfectly coiffed blond hair.

Fuck that guy. He didn't matter. What mattered was getting Christmas perfect for him and Matt. Their first one in their own place was extra special, and Aedan was woefully behind on his schedule. Still, it would have been better *not* to have been spoken to like that.

A tut came from his right hip. Aedan looked down to see a girl of about eight years of age shaking her head.

"Elsa was a snow queen. Not a fairy." The girl pushed her glasses up her nose and looked up at Aedan. "He doesn't know *anything.*"

Aedan had to laugh, immediately feeling a little comforted. "No, he certainly doesn't."

The girl sighed. "I hate shopping," she said.

In that moment, Aedan had to agree. "Sometimes it can be fun. Are you with your parents?" he asked.

The girl pushed her glasses up again, like she wasn't used to them. "Yeah. My dad." She pointed at a fraught looking man a few feet away agonising over two different scarves. "He *always* leaves mum's present 'til Christmas Eve." She narrowed her eyes at Aedan. "Did you leave your girlfriend's present until now too?"

Aedan sighed at his new friend. "I got my boyfriend a perfect present, actually," he said sadly. "But it was coming from America and it didn't arrive in time."

"Oh no!" said the girl with the kind of earnest concern only kids could muster. "So you're looking for a backup."

Aedan nodded, feeling glum. "And a bunch of other things. We haven't even decorated our tree yet."

The logical side of his brain argued that this late in the day, the tree didn't matter. Only Matt's present mattered, so he should get that sorted first. But the tree was part of the whole Christmas experience. Just as much as the food and the games and the same old festive films they played on the TV every year. It all added up to make Christmas the best time of year, so Aedan didn't want to miss a single thing.

Matt's present not showing up had very much put a spanner in the works.

The little girl patted his coat sleeve. "Don't worry. Like my mum says *every* year, it's not the present that matters in the end. It's the thought that counts."

Aedan arched his eyebrow at her dad. They really were two fugly scarves.

"Thank you," he said.

She did have a point. But Christmas was an extra special time for him and Matt. It was also their anniversary on the

27th. Aedan was extremely disappointed his gift hadn't arrived in time, but there surely had to be something else he could get in London in the next few hours.

It wasn't even the most expensive present. The proper gift was the one he had sorted for their anniversary. But like the girl said, he'd put a lot of thought into the one for Christmas Day, and due to its nature, it wouldn't do much good if it arrived after that.

The little girl's dad chewed on his lip and rubbed the cheap material between his fingers and thumbs. Someone ought to at least do well in tomorrow's gift giving.

Aedan popped a hand on his hip. "What does your mum like doing for hobbies?" he asked the girl.

"Like, when she's not at work?" she said, frowning. "Umm...reading books. Real books. She likes the smell of them. Otherwise, he'd get her an eReader." She rolled her eyes, apparently having heard her dad lament this fact many times.

Aedan broke into a big smile. That was too easy. "Okay," he said.

He put down his ornaments and pulled a receipt out of one of his bags from the presents he'd already bought. No one would want to return chocolates, of that he was confident.

"Tell your dad to get bubble bath," he said, starting to scribble a list on the back of the receipt for her. "A 'Do Not Disturb' sign, one of those hand painted wine goblets from the glass ware section over there, candles, bookmarks from that craft fair on the street outside, and if he's got any budget left, book tokens. Sound good?"

The little girl's eyes were wide as she took the list after he finished writing it. "Yeah," she said, then grinned up at him. "You're really good at this."

He shrugged. If he was really good at it, he wouldn't have left everything until the last minute. "Have a merry Christmas," he said to her.

"You too. Good luck with your boyfriend's present, I'm sure you'll do great!" She waved and skipped back over to her dad, proudly brandishing the list Aedan had written.

He slipped away into the crowd, preferring to remain anonymous for his good deed. Hopefully the girl's mum would like her present.

Aedan looked down at the three blue crystals he'd picked back up again, deciding he might as well buy them. He had a few decorations for their new tree now, but not even half the amount he'd hoped. He'd already been through most of the shops on the main high street and it was starting to get dark outside.

He huffed. Enough moping. He could get on the tube and go to the shopping mall out east. That was only a couple of stops away from their home and he still had several hours before the shops would close at ten o'clock. He really hoped he wouldn't be out until then; he still had everything to wrap, after all. But the thought of trekking back down the long length of Oxford Street to go through the stores again made him want to cry.

He looked down at the bags in his hands. He'd gotten presents for most people on his list, but none of them felt like complete gifts yet. They were all impersonal and generic items; perfume, makeup, chocolate, soap, socks. Not that there was anything wrong with any of those. It just screamed to Aedan of not putting enough effort in.

That made his mind up. He was going to travel to the other set of shops and try again. Maybe a seasonal coffee along the way would perk him up.

He just needed to dig deep and find his usual Christmas

spirit. He knew it was lurking about somewhere. It just needed a little help to find its way out.

Hopefully, some time before tomorrow. He was not going to be the Grinch who ruined Christmas.

2

IN THE BLEAK MIDWINTER

Westfield in Stratford was a relatively new shopping complex situated at the end of the Jubilee Line in East London. It meant Aedan had to travel past his home stop at Canning Town, but it was only two stations further. He was fuelled by a gingerbread soya latte with extra marshmallows, the sugar and caffeine doing wonders for his enthusiasm and, once he hopped off the tube, his walking speed.

"You can do this," he muttered to himself. "You can do it. Just focus."

He glanced at his watch. Seven o'clock. That meant he had three hours still to try and improve on the gifts he'd managed to get so far, particularly for Matt.

He'd not failed completely on Oxford Street. He'd got Matt some fun socks, aftershave, a couple of DVDs and sweets in ridiculous Christmas flavours that came from America. They weren't as personal as the original present Aedan had ordered, but they were something for Matt to open in the morning at least.

Aedan walked through the front doors of the shopping centre and breathed in the warm air. One of the usual

Christmas songs was pumping out over the sound system and the floor was packed with people darting between stores.

From experience, Aedan knew he could traverse one side of the building to the other in five minutes. There were three levels of shops, making it much easier to get between everything, unlike Oxford Street. He shook his head. He should have just come here first.

Never mind, he had no time to waste. First, he decided to go to John Lewis at the opposite end of the shopping centre. That was the same department store he'd been in on Oxford Street, and he hoped they'd maybe have more stock of the blue ice crystals he so desperately wanted for the tree.

On the way, he could see if there was anything better that caught his eye to add to his presents.

He'd not done all that badly. He didn't have that many people to buy for after all; it was mostly just Matt's mum and sister and the few members of his extended family. Aedan hardly had anything to do with his own family these days; he got the impression they much preferred it that way. He wouldn't even see most of them over the holiday period, so that saved him time, money and aggravation at least.

Matt's family were different though. They had welcomed him into their fold with open arms and he cared very much about them.

He and Matt were driving down to Matt's mum's house first thing the next morning. Her home was just about big enough to sleep them all comfortably tomorrow night, but Matt had insisted that they wake up in their flat for the first Christmas since they'd moved in.

They were still pouring their hearts and paycheques into making the space their own. As a new build, it didn't have structural issues or anything, but both of them had all kinds of ideas about fitted wardrobes and kitchen cabinets and light fittings. Matt enjoyed upcycling old bits of furniture and Aedan loved painting walls and matching up art and knick-knacks to colour schemes on the walls.

So that was why Matt had insisted they take a little bit of time to themselves to swap Christmas presents in the home they had worked so hard to create over the past few months. However, Aedan secretly suspected he just wanted to give Aedan and him some time alone more than anything else.

That was fine by Aedan. December had been an utter blur, and the idea of taking the early part of the morning for just the two of them sounded heavenly. That was, if Aedan could get everything he needed before the shops closed tonight.

He and Matt had actually sorted Dawn, Matt's mum, out with her present weeks ago. They'd bought her and her new partner, Keith, tickets to see Les Misérables at the West End. But all they had to open tomorrow was a printout of the tickets.

Dawn deserved more than that. Aedan would have normally handmade her a card with plenty of glitter to put the tickets in. But between his job and all the work on the flat, he'd not managed to get the time. Maybe he should get her an extra present now, just from him? A pretty pair of earrings or a nice top she could wear for New Year's?

Tilly too, Matt's sister. They'd got her a selection of skincare products from Charlotte Tilbury that Aedan knew she would love, but he still wanted to buy her something fun as well.

Keith was a nice guy, but Aedan had known Dawn and Tilly for years, ever since they had welcomed Aedan into the family as Matt's boyfriend. They had been kinder and more supportive than Aedan's family had even been. Even their dog, Buster, loved Aedan more than he suspected his own parents did.

Aedan had at least got Buster some fun, festive treats and

a new coat to keep him warm on his walks. That was the only present that could be considered complete.

As he wandered through Accessorize Aedan made up his mind that Dawn and Tilly both needed something else, maybe a gift they wouldn't be likely to buy themselves. Nothing extravagant, just something to add a little 'glitter on the garland' as his Aunt Eileen always said.

Used to say.

Fuck.

He hated when it crept up on him like that, out of nowhere. He pushed out of the jewellery store to the edge of the crowded walkway to grip onto the railing. He looked down to the lower floors and tried to catch his breath.

The tears came anyway, but he hoped no one would notice as he hastily brushed them away with the back of his hand.

He didn't have much in the way of relations he was close to. He got on well with his sister and her husband, but they didn't have a lot in common. The rest of his extremely large family either tolerated him or weren't shy about showing how much they were disgusted by him for being gay.

Eileen was different; just as bright and effervescent as he was. Never giving a shit what anybody thought, marching to her own beat, following her own star.

Or at least, she had been.

Cancer was such an evil fucking bitch. How could it take someone so free-spirited and gregarious, then reduce them to a weak and sickly creature so fast?

Maybe it was better if you had more warning. Which hurt more? Taking months or even years to prepare yourself for the inevitable, or to have your last days snatched away within a matter of weeks? It could have been worse, Aedan supposed as people brushed past him, jostling his shopping bags. It could have been a car crash or something.

At least he got to say goodbye.

At least Eileen got to see Aedan happy, happy with Matt especially. See them follow their dreams and move to London. She never got to visit the flat they bought, but she left him an inheritance specifically to help with their deposit.

He'd told himself that this would be fine. That she was there in spirit this Christmas, still sprinkling her glitter everywhere. But maybe that was another reason he had put off holiday preparations for so long. He didn't want it to really go ahead without her.

He took a shuddery breath. He had to, though. There was no bringing her back, but he still had people he cared for. They needed to see how much he appreciated them, and he wasn't going to do that with mediocre gifts.

With one last huff, he carefully rubbed his face, trying not to smudge the eyeliner, and carried on down to the other end of the shopping centre. He would honour Eileen and get Matt's family members a little something extra each, give them that sparkle to make them smile.

At least money wasn't the concern it used to be. Aedan's job as an I.T. consultant for one of the financial companies in the city centre meant his wage was decent. So while before he would have had that to worry about as well, now he could afford to be a little frivolous.

The spring came back in his step. He assured himself he was almost done, at least with the presents. He just needed to think of something special for Matt to top off the generic gifts he had already got, then find some pretty trinkets for Dawn and Tilly.

Aedan smiled to himself as he entered John Lewis. "Just hang in there a little longer," he murmured to himself. He rolled his tired shoulders and wandered deeper into the department store.

The Christmas section was a large display right in the

middle of the store. They wanted to entice as many people in as possible with the sparkles, like magpies. It always worked on Aedan, he appreciated with a chuckle.

But his mirth didn't last. After several solid minutes of searching, he finally found the label for where the highly coveted blue hanging crystals should have been. Except they were entirely sold out.

Aedan swore, loudly enough for the old dear the other side of the display to jump. "Sorry," said Aedan, but she was already bustling off, shaking her head.

He sighed. Perhaps there were some other similar decorations left? He poked through the rack, hunting for anything else that looked icy and glittery. But it seemed all that was left was in red with holly and berries.

Aedan shook his head. He should just forget about it. They probably wouldn't even get time to decorate the tree tonight anyway. Matt was working a late shift and wouldn't be home until ten or eleven o'clock. Aedan would be lucky at this rate to be home by then, let alone get his presents wrapped up. He'd wasted almost an hour in Westfield already; he needed to up his game.

Best to forget about buying new decorations now. He had to sort Matt's final gift, get a few extra little presents for his family, then Aedan could grab whatever paper was left from the card shop, a load of sticky tape, then hit the Marks and Spencer food hall on the way out.

His plan was to get several packets of their delicious, fancy party food selection. Mini brie and cranberry tartlets, honey roasted sausage bites, crispy breaded mushrooms, maybe a wheel of camembert to put in the oven and vegetable crudités to dunk in it, not to mention some tasty fresh bread and crisps in the ridiculous flavours they put out just for Christmas. Aedan's mouth watered at just the thought of it.

He pushed his way back towards the shopping mall concourse. He'd had a brainwave that he could get Matt a nice, mid-range watch, seeing as his old one still had Batman on it. Aedan actually loved that stupid watch, but it would be good for Matt to have a grown up one for events or going out.

Aedan checked his own watch. Eight o'clock. Perfect. He still had two hours until the shops closed, and Matt wasn't likely to be back until around eleven.

Except, as he walked past Cath Kidston on his way to the jewellery store, the shutters rattled down beside him.

He stopped. Why the hell where they closing? All the shops were open until ten o'clock in the run up to Christmas. In fact, some places stayed open until eleven. Aedan snapped his head around…just in time to see Mamas & Papas babywear also closing down their grills.

"What the fuck?" he whispered.

No, no, *no*, this couldn't be happening! He pushed through the crown towards Earnest Jones. Although, it did suddenly seem like there were a lot less people around.

"Excuse me," he said, breathlessly as he reached the jewellery shop. The shutters weren't down at least, but there was only one guy amidst all the watches, necklaces and rings, and he was holding a cabinet key as he looked up at Aedan's greeting. "Are you still open?"

The sales assistant looked over at Aedan sympathetically. "I'm afraid not."

"But," Aedan spluttered. "Everywhere's supposed to be open until ten?"

The guy shook his head. "Not on Christmas Eve," he said. "You'll be lucky to find anywhere open past eight tonight."

The tears sprung into Aedan's eyes, but he did his best to blink them back. "Okay," he managed to stammer. "Uh, thank you."

He turned and stumbled back onto the walkway, his many bags bashing against his knees. In horror, he watched as all the shops in his eyeline dragged their shutters down a few feet, encouraging those still inside to leave, or slammed them all the way to the floor so no one else could get in.

He was fucked. He was totally fucked.

None of his presents were complete, especially not Matt's, which was pitifully inadequate. They didn't have any food in or festive wrapping paper. Their local newsagents would probably be open until late like usual so he could maybe grab *something*. But what did that matter when he was missing everything else to make the next few days special?

He'd wasted all that time on the stupid decorations and buying coffee when he should have been racing around trying to achieve everything he'd failed to over the past month.

Christmas was ruined. And it was all his fault.

3

MISTLETOE AND WINE

AEDAN MADE HIS WAY BACK TO THE TUBE STATION IN A DAZE. He felt numb. Of course, there was a small, logical part of his brain that knew this wasn't really the end of the world. But it really felt like it as he followed the other shoppers as they squashed into the train carriage.

He was going to be mortified when Matt opened just a few, lacklustre things tomorrow. He kept reminding himself that his original present wasn't very expensive, so it didn't matter that he hadn't spent that much money today. But that gift had been so personal to Matt. Aedan had been so sure he'd allowed enough time for postage…

He gritted his teeth as the train doors closed and people pressed into him from all sides. As this was the start of the line, it was usually quite empty. But everyone had evidently left Westfield at the same time, so were all trying to board the tube at once.

It was fine. Matt would be back so late they probably wouldn't eat or drink much anyway. They could decorate the tree next year and make the flat look pretty. He could hopefully get wrapping paper from the corner shop on the way home.

But that didn't solve the problem that he hadn't got people what he wanted. He stared miserably at his reflection in the window as the tube tore through the night. This section of the line was above ground, and he tried to focus on the building lights in the distance. But he kept coming back to his own face as he tried not to cry.

People were going to think he didn't care about them when that couldn't be further from the truth. He loved his inherited family more than anything and he'd let them down.

By the time he pushed his way off at Canning Town Station he felt thoroughly wretched. But there was nothing he could do, no solution that would fix this. He'd promised Matt he'd sort everything, and he'd simply run out of time.

Aedan rubbed the back of his neck, under his old faithful chunky knit scarf, and sighed. He'd just have to explain what had happened to Matt and offer to take him shopping in the sales. Matt wasn't materialistic, he'd probably love what Aedan had bought for him. But that didn't make Aedan feel any less like he'd spoiled everything.

It was only a five-minute walk from the station to Aedan and Matt's apartment, but Aedan's thoughts were churning so much it felt like longer. Especially with all the heavy bags he had in his hands.

The trouble was, as bizarre as it might sound, the nicer Matt's family were in comparison to Aedan's own, the harder he found it. It just reminded him of what he didn't have. Especially around the holidays, but now this year was even worse than usual because he didn't even have Aunt Eileen.

He was so grateful to have Matt's family. Hopefully they would understand that this year he'd just dropped the ball a little. He tried to apply logic; *of course* they would get it. They had treated him as part of the family ever since Aedan had shown up at their doorstep seven years ago, back when Matt was just his best friend.

That was the best decision Aedan had ever made. Never in his wildest dreams would he have dared hope that one day Matt would reciprocate the love Aedan had carried around since they'd met on the first day of senior school. He needed to remember how lucky he was.

But his mind was filled with thoughts as dark as the sky above him. He *was* lucky, he just needed to show Matt he knew that. But instead Aedan had bought him and his family mediocre gifts. He'd not bothered to decorate the artificial tree that had been sitting in their living room the past week. He'd skipped out on several Christmas parties, unable to face smiling at so many people when he felt hollow inside.

He needed to keep sparkling for Eileen, to honour her memory. She hadn't been restrained by their family's expectations either and lived her life to its fullest. It sucked beyond compare that it had been cut far too short, but Aedan needed to find it within him to keep going.

The air inside the building's lobby was blissfully warm as he pushed his way through the front doors with his bags. Matt would be home in a couple of hours and Aedan wanted to do his best to cheer up by then.

He loved Matt with all his heart and soul. No matter how disappointed Aedan was with his efforts today, he was going to find as many ways to show that as he could.

He waited for the lift to get him to the right floor and made his way down the hall to their door. He juggled his bags to get his keys out of his pocket to let himself into the flat. They were on the third floor of the new building and had a pretty decent view of east London from their balcony. There was an even better view from the large communal garden on the roof; you could see Canary Wharf and the

Queen Elizabeth Olympic stadium and even the Shard in London Bridge from up there.

They had been very lucky to snag one of the apartments in the development when they did. Thanks to Eileen's generous inheritance in her will, they had been able to afford the deposit and get themselves on the property ladder. That wasn't something a lot of people in their twenties in London could boast, even with good jobs like Aedan and Matt had.

Over the years they had done numerous house shares with other students and professionals, but nothing could compare with the feeling of getting the keys to your own place at the end of the summer. To step through your own front door and know that no matter what, you were safe and content and with the person you loved was undoubtedly one of Aedan's greatest joys in life. So despite his miserable shopping trip, he tried to let go of the tension in his shoulders and relax as he swung open the door.

Except…the hallway wasn't dark like he expected. He blinked at the white fairy lights strung up at the top of the walls on both sides, leading to the bedroom and open kitchen/living room space. The air that wafted out from the flat was warmer than he would have expected, and – what was that incredible smell?

"Hello?" he called out uncertainly as he closed the front door behind him. It sounded like the TV was on, but Matt couldn't be home, could he?

The noise from the TV suddenly stopped and within a second Matt slid out into the hall on his socks. He was in joggers rather than the jeans he wore to work and one of his signature hideous Christmas jumpers that Aedan adored. This one had a picture of Jesus on in a party hat, holding a balloon with a badge that read 'Birthday Boy!' on.

His face lit up at the sight of Aedan. "Babe!" he cried,

dashing over to hug him. "I was starting to get worried, why didn't you answer your phone?"

Aedan dropped his bags to the floor and threw his arms around his boyfriend's neck, chocking back a sob. "It's been in my pocket," he confessed. He'd not even been listening to music like usual, such was his melancholy. Thinking about it, he hadn't checked the damn thing for hours. "I'm so sorry. Were you very worried? What are you doing home?"

He leaned back and looked into Matt's blueish-grey eyes. He was so gorgeous it made Aedan's heart skip.

"They let us go home early," Matt said in delight. "No filming over the Christmas break, so it makes sense."

Having got a degree in history, Matt had done the sensible thing and also got his teaching qualifications. But after a year of working himself ragged, his fortune had taken an unexpected turn. Last year, he'd happened to bump into someone at a party who worked for the BBC as a writer on a historical drama, and they just so happened to be looking for a new historian as a fact checker to liaise with them on a regular basis. Now Matt worked on a couple of different productions and couldn't be happier. He could always go back into teaching; he'd found it extremely rewarding after all, even though it was exhausting. But for now, Aedan was beyond proud that his fabulous man was getting to experience such an exciting career.

Matt always insisted that Aedan was the gorgeous and fabulous one. Aedan did his best to make sure Matt knew that wasn't the case.

"I'm so happy you're here," Aedan said, horrified when his voice cracked. He hugged Matt again to try and disguise his upset, but of course Matt noticed.

"Hey," he said gently as he rubbed Aedan's back. "What's the matter? Everything okay?"

Aedan whined. "Oh, babe!" he sobbed. "I've ruined Christmas!"

"Hey, hey," said Matt urgently. "What on earth are you talking about?"

Aedan screwed up his eyes as the tears leaked out. He was probably getting his makeup everywhere. "All my presents are rubbish," he stammered and clung harder to Matt. "I didn't get any food, I forgot the wrapping paper." He only just realised that in his dark mood he failed to pop into the corner shop on the way back to get some. "I never decorated the flat and…and…"

He hiccupped back his distress as best he could, but Matt was hugging him fiercely. "You are such a prat," he said fondly and kissed his check. "You should have just checked your phone. Come here, let me show you my surprise."

Gently, he eased Aedan out of his coat and waited while he kicked his shoes off. Then he took his hand, and together, they both padded into the main living space of the flat in their socks.

Aedan gasped.

The tree was covered in lights and tinsel and garlands and a whole hodgepodge of ornaments. Garlands were strung over the mirrors and framed movie posters they had around the room, and the cabinet surfaces had a number of tacky holiday figurines scattered all over. Where Aedan had envisaged a pristine, ice-blue winter wonderland, there was a mess of colour. Instead of the elegant crystal decorations Aedan had in one of his bags, there looked to be a whole nativity from the pound shop down the road as well as many other painfully cheap-looking ornaments. There were cross-eyed robins and uneven snowmen and the garlands were so poorly made they looked like genuine fire-hazards.

It was possibly the most beautiful thing Aedan had ever seen.

"Oh," he said, touching his fingers to his mouth. "You've got absolutely no taste whatsoever, have you?"

Matt beamed at him. "Does that mean you like it?" he asked, rocking on the balls of his feet.

"I fucking love it," Aedan cried, grabbing his boyfriend and pulling him into a fierce hug. This time he didn't bother to try and stop the tears that soaked into the shoulder of the awful jumper.

He should have known he didn't need it all matching and pristine for it to be perfect. He just needed Matt; and everything about this glorious, ghastly display screamed Matt Bartlett.

"I'm sorry," said Matt.

Aedan hiccupped and blinked in surprise. "Why on earth would you be sorry?" He pulled back to stare at Matt in honest confusion.

Matt stroked his checks, wiping away the tears. "Because I know we've both been busy, but I let you think you had to do all this by yourself. I should have realised sooner how important it was, and helped."

Aedan shook his head and buried his face against Matt's neck again. "I wanted to do it all."

"I know," said Matt fondly. "But you shouldn't have to."

Aedan nodded. "This really is perfect though," he insisted. "Thank you."

Matt kissed his hair. "You don't need to thank me, gorgeous. But I'm so happy you like it."

"I love it," Aedan mumbled into his neck. "I love you."

"Love you too," Matt said with a chuckle, swaying Aedan back and forth. "Now come here. Let's cheer you up."

Aedan allowed himself to be led over to the kitchen. There was mulled wine simmering gently in a pan on the hob, a baked camembert bubbling on a low heat in the oven, and an assortment of the very party foods that Aedan had hoped to get himself. Spring rolls and chicken goujons and breaded mushrooms had all been kept warm in preparation for Aedan's return home.

"Oh, babe," he said shakily. He wiped his eyes as Matt handed him a mug of mulled wine that warmed his insides from the first sip. "This is amazing."

Matt brushed some of Aedan's hair back where it had come loose from the wax. "Do you want to tell me what's on your mind before we start eating?" he asked. "It will all keep, I promise. But if you'd rather not talk about it, I understand."

Aedan sighed. He took Matt by the hand and led him to the sofa. "I don't know," he said to procrastinate a little longer. He sipped his wine and snuggled against Matt's side. It looked like he'd been watching Die Hard from the image paused on the TV screen, and Aedan highly approved. "I fucked up all the presents," he blurted out.

Matt leaned his head against Aedan's. "I'm sure you didn't," he said kindly.

But Aedan shook his head. "I just feel like I got nothing special, and yours..." he sighed. "Yours didn't come at all. It was only a silly little something. Your real gift is your anniversary present. But I wanted you to open this tomorrow and I'm so sorry and-"

"*Babe*," interrupted Matt firmly. "Calm down. Not to be rude, but I don't give a crap about presents. I care about you. If I just have you tomorrow morning, then that's okay with me."

Aedan managed a wet laugh and rubbed the tears from his face. His eyeliner was almost totally gone, he was sure. "Okay," he said softly. That had been his thinking with the anniversary present, which was a cheeky long weekend in Paris he'd managed to get a sweet deal on. Spending time with Matt was always the best gift. "I didn't get anything for your family," he added weakly.

Matt kissed his temple. "What are you talking about? We got Mum and Tilly stuff together. What's in those bags?"

He jutted his chin to the front door. Aedan shrugged. "Stuff for your nan, and your aunt, uncle and cousins. Oh, and Buster. But, I wanted to get other stuff for your mum and Tilly. It just seems all naff and no good." He tucked his head further down Matt's chest so he wouldn't have to look at him.

Matt stroked his back. "But you made all those mix CDs a while ago, didn't you?"

Aedan stilled. "Oh my god," he said. "Oh my *god*, I forgot all about those." He looked tearfully up at Matt. "Oh that's perfect and amazing!"

"See," Matt said with a grin. "Everyone will love those."

"And they're personal," Aedan said in agreement.

Matt brushed his hair back again and smiled. "A little glitter on the garland."

That made Aedan think of Eileen, but he tried to swallow it down. "I still have to wrap everything," he said. That seemed like such a monumental task with him so low on energy, and he had to blink back more tears.

"I'll help you," said Matt cheerfully. "It'll be even more fun when we're good and smashed on mulled wine. Tilly will be very impressed with our combined skills."

Aedan managed to give him a real laugh. Matt's sister loved to tease him about his total ineptitude when it came to wrapping presents. They hadn't seen her in so long. She had just started her doctorate and was immersed in her PhD research. It was going to be fantastic to spend the next few days with her.

"Okay," whispered Aedan again.

They sat there for a while. Aedan suspected Matt was allowing him to think. He probably realised Aedan wasn't done talking.

"It's like," he said eventually, after half his wine was gone and his head started buzzing pleasantly, "I want to remember Eileen by still dousing everything in glitter, like we always do. But…she's not here anymore, and it feels like the more I try to be festive, the more disrespectful it feels."

Matt sighed. "I wondered if that was it."

In all honestly, it wasn't like Aedan had seen his aunt all the time. Maybe a few times a year if they were lucky. But he always felt they were kindred spirits and he'd secretly hoped one day she might have found her true love too and built her life with someone.

But that wasn't Eileen's way. She travelled and wrote her blogs and articles and would rather have drifted through Asia doing odd jobs and partying rather than settle down. The whole world was her true love.

"Do you think she'd be disappointed we used her money to buy this place?" he asked, voicing his fear for the first time.

"No," said Matt surprisingly quickly. He said it confidently, and kissed Aedan's head again. "No, babe. I know she was into all that hippy stuff," he said with a chuckle, "but she specifically wanted to help us out in this way. She knew how much it would mean to you."

Aedan heard what Matt didn't say. He knew it was important for Aedan to have a brick and mortar home after growing up in the instability of an Irish traveller camp. Caravans had been way of his people for generations. But Aedan had enough uncertainty to contend with being gay in such a hyper-masculine environment. With being poor and bullied at school. With being beaten at home and heckled on the street for being a fucking poof.

Matt had always been his stability, even when they were just friends. But becoming boyfriends had been one of the best things to happen in Aedan's life. Eileen knew that. She knew how much this start meant to them. Even if it wasn't the same sort of dream she had. They were both rebels and outcasts, just in different ways.

"She did know how much it would mean to me," Aedan agreed. "To us."

He sighed. He needed to let his guilt go. It was okay to keep on living without her. It was okay that it hurt. But...it was also okay that with each day, it hurt just that tiny bit less.

"I don't want to spoil Christmas," he said, taking a big, shaky breath in.

Matt squeezed his shoulder. "You're not at all, I promise. Do you fancy eating now?"

"Oh my god, I'm starving," Aedan groaned and laughed. "Thanks, gorgeous."

"It was no trouble to cook," said Matt.

But Aedan pulled him to his feet and cuddled him close. "I wasn't talking about the food," he said into the lovely, ugly jumper.

4

JOY TO THE WORLD

As the evening went on, Aedan managed to gradually relax.

Matt dished up the food he'd miraculously managed to keep warm despite Aedan not responding to all his calls and texts. When Aedan guiltily checked his phone, his heart panged as he saw all the photos Matt had sent of his progress with the tree and the food as he put it in the oven. He was such a dork. But that was why Aedan loved him so.

Of course, Matt didn't care he'd been ignored, only that Aedan was home now and okay. And after their chat, he was feeling better than ever.

As Matt plated up all the scrumptious smelling goodies, he insisted Aedan add his few decorations to the tree around the ones he'd already hung. The troublesome blue icicles looked perfectly at home amidst all Matt's jaunty Santas and plastic pug dogs wearing their own terrible Christmas jumpers. There were even some baubles that Matt had attached cardboard cut-outs of Miley Cyrus to so that she looked like she was swinging on her wrecking ball.

Aedan chuckled and went back over to Matt, kissing his check fondly as he joined him in tucking in to their feast.

Matt insisted on flicking Die Hard back to the start. "I'd only got about twenty minutes in," he said. Aedan could tell from the shot that had been paused on the screen that he wasn't telling the truth. But it made Matt happy to watch the film from the beginning because he could share it with Aedan. And that made Aedan happy.

They did indeed get a little merry on the hot, spiced wine. When Die Hard finished, they began wrapping up their mountain of presents. Matt put on Frozen and the two of them sang along to the songs loudly. Aedan hoped their neighbours had already gone out to the suburbs to visit their families. But even if they hadn't, it wasn't enough to stop him bellowing 'Let It Go' at the top of his lungs.

When they had all the presents laid out in front of them, Aedan realised they had done a pretty good job between the two of them. He couldn't believe he'd forgotten all about those CDs he'd made that weekend back in November. But that made everything better. To him, music was one of the best gifts you could ever give someone else. The songs he'd chosen to share with each of Matt's family members might very well stay with them for years to come.

He and Matt bumped shoulders and touched knees as they sat on the floor amidst a mountain of paper, tape, tags and presents. Aedan kept glancing over at Matt as he worked, smiling to himself. This was what Christmas was about. Not gifts; people.

"What?" Matt asked.

"Nothing," said Aedan, taking another sip of wine. "Shut up and wrap faster, elf."

Matt laughed and did as he was told, but only after tackling Aedan for a kiss.

Matt's technique for wrapping presents was horrendous.

His family's dog Buster would probably do a better job with his paws. But for once, Aedan imitated his sloppy style. Not every gift had to be perfectly and evenly wrapped with bows and ribbons on top. They'd be there all evening if they did that, and quite frankly, from the way Matt kept looking over at him, Aedan could tell he probably had other plans for their night.

When the last package was ensconced in the bright paper Matt had bought, the two of them separated to wrap their gifts to each other. Aedan had already stashed Matt's gifts away in the bedroom, and Matt said he was okay to stay in the lounge.

This was the last thing he had to do tonight, Aedan promised himself as he sat on the bed to work. Matt had even done a load of washing for them in preparation for going away. All he had to do tomorrow was pack his toothbrush and some underwear.

He sighed as he looked at the presents laid out before him. They still weren't the most impressive bunch, but they didn't seem like the utter failure he'd built them up to be earlier. He'd still take Matt out shopping for something once the shops were back open, but in the meantime, tomorrow morning shouldn't be a total embarrassment. It depended what Matt had got him, he supposed.

It took about twenty minutes to get everything wrapped, and he even bothered to stick some shiny bows on them for added effect. "There," he said happily to himself and gave a little clap. "All done."

He hopped off the bed and raising his arms up, stretching and popping his back. Hopefully Matt was done with his lot as well now.

When he turned to look out the window he got a surprise. "Oh!" he said out loud, watching the soft, white snowflakes drift down in the darkness. He stepped up to the glass, touching the cold surface as he peered out into the night. Most of his plans might not have come to fruition. But a white Christmas was something he couldn't have predicted, not in England. Normally they just got rain. This was perfect in a way he couldn't have engineered if he'd tried.

Maybe, some things were just better when they happened naturally.

Grinning like a fool, he scooped up Matt's pile of presents and nudged his way through the door back into the lounge. Matt was standing with his back to him as Aedan crossed the room and placed his packages by the tree. Matt was also watching the snow.

He turned and looked excitedly at Aedan when he heard the rustling of presents. "Look!" he whispered.

Aedan bounded back up to his feet and stood next to him. "I know," he said. He took a mouthful of wine from the glass he'd left on the table. It was lukewarm now, but it still tasted good.

Matt took the glass from him and had a sip himself. "Come on," he said, his eyes twinkling. "Let's go take a look from the roof."

Aedan laughed. He wanted to protest that it was freezing cold and Matt was crazy. But then he remembered how their very first kiss had been in the snow and he was soon jamming his feet into his boots and winding his massive scarf around his neck.

They giggled like children as they raced hand in hand along the corridor towards the stairwell. They could have taken the lift, but there was something more clandestine about sneaking round the back.

"Shush!" hissed Matt drunkenly, pressing his finger to his plump lips. Aedan batted his hand away and kissed them.

"You shush," he told him with a grin.

This was what his aunt wanted. She wanted him to live

his life. To have silly little midnight adventures with the man he loved. To have a home where he felt secure, a place he could be proud of. A job that wasn't just a job, it was a career he cared about. To have a life where he, and Matt, chased their dreams.

Aedan let Matt pull him to the middle of the landscaped rooftop. It was deserted apart from the snow falling all around them. Aedan fell into Matt's arms, although Aedan was actually the taller of the two, so he let Matt snuggle against his shoulder.

For a while they swayed together, enjoying the cold snow touching their overly hot skin. Aedan hadn't realised how warm the flat had got from all their cooking, as well as their own body temperature rising from eating said food and drinking the lovely, hot wine.

"I love you, babe," he murmured.

Matt smiled against his neck. "Love you too, gorgeous."

Matt's kisses started sweetly, trailing up Aedan's neck and along his jaw. His hands slipped under Aedan's coat and jumper, finding his ticklish abs. Aedan was pretty sure he'd put on ten pounds from all the festive cheer he'd indulged in, despite not going to as many parties as usual. But he knew Matt wouldn't care. He loved him whether he was buff or skinny or even a little chubby.

Aedan knew this, because that's exactly how he felt about Matt.

He knew Matt's body as well as his own after all these years. Every curve and angle, dip and crest. To Aedan, he was utterly perfect.

"Let's go back downstairs," he said as Matt's lips found his own.

Matt hummed, but he didn't move. "Just a minute," he said, smiling against his mouth. Aedan was happy to oblige.

They kissed gently, not moving into anything more

urgent, just perfectly at ease with each other. Until Matt pulled carefully away and checked his old Batman watch.

"Merry Christmas," he said with a grin.

Aedan moved Matt's wrist to see the time for himself. It had indeed just gone past midnight.

"Merry Christmas, babe," he said.

He used to call everyone that. Now, he reserved the title only for Matt.

5

MERRY AND BRIGHT

They stayed up on the roof for a while, alternating between watching the snow silently falling and kissing each other tenderly. But soon, the kisses became more urgent, passion brewing between them. Once they began to shiver, Aedan tugged on Matt's coat.

"Seeing as it's now Christmas," he said, fluttering his eyelashes, "I think you should open your present."

Matt licked his lips and wrapped his arms tighter around Aedan's back. "I thought my present didn't arrive?"

"Well," said Aedan, rolling his eyes. "I forgot that you already have the best gift you could ever wish for right here." He grinned and wiggled his eyebrows, mischief clear in his words.

But Matt looked very serious as his gaze raked up and down Aedan's body. "Damn right I do," he said. "And seeing as I've been oh so good, I think it's only fair I get to open it. Now."

Aedan's heart rate sped up. He nodded, pulling Matt back towards the door that led back into the apartment complex.

By the time they were in the stairwell they were kissing

desperately, hands roaming under clothes, seeking warm skin to touch. It was a miracle neither of them tripped as they fumbled their way down the steps.

"I hope no one comes out thinking it's Father Christmas making all this noise," said Aedan giddily.

Matt urged him through the door back onto their corridor. "I'd better get you into bed quick then," he said, his voice husky.

No matter how many times they did this, Aedan still came undone every time like it was the first. Except this was better than the first time they made love. They'd been young and clumsy with more enthusiasm than skill. Now, after countless tumbles between the sheets, they knew just how to drive each other crazy.

The building was safe enough that they'd not bothered to lock the door for their little venture upstairs. Therefore, when Matt pushed Aedan's back against it, it opened easily with a click.

Matt paused to lock it behind them for the night, giving Aedan the chance to flick off the main lights, just leaving them with the glow of the white fairy lights Matt had strung up that afternoon. It looked like Aedan's winter wonderland after all like that.

He yanked Matt back to him once the door was secure, exploring his mouth with his tongue. Between them, they first divested themselves of their outdoor wear, then Aedan tackled the wonderful, ugly Christmas jumper.

Every now and again, he would remember that Matt had never slept with anyone else but him. Not that he felt there was anything wrong with sowing one's wild oats. But there was something undeniably special about knowing that no one else had ever been granted the precious gift of touching Matt when he was completely naked. Vulnerable and pure and beautiful.

Aedan snorted. Okay, he was maybe still a bit drunk. But that didn't mean he wasn't thinking honestly. Matt's body was all his. Equally, his body was all Matt's. Aedan considered the guys he'd been with all those years ago as simply practice. He and Matt had grown and learned so much together. Yet, every time they made love it was different, even if it was only in tiny ways.

Aedan smiled against Matt's lips as they stumbled over the threshold, their clothes peeling away as they neared the bed. Their bodies had changed over the years, bulking out from those scrawny teenagers they used to be.

"Babe," Aedan rasped.

Matt kissed down his throat and along his clavicle. Aedan slipped his fingers through Matt's thick, brown hair, allowing himself to be pushed down onto the mattress. Matt straddled his hips and pulled Aedan's t-shirt – the last layer of clothing on his chest – over his head and tossed the garment on the floor. He had a hungry look in his eyes.

"Yes, gorgeous?" Matt asked, a teasing glint in his eye.

"Nothing," Aedan said with a grin. "Just wanted to say it." He pawed at Matt's own t-shirt. "Off please. More hot body."

Matt smirked and did as he was tasked, revealing his wide chest and delicious pecs. He wasn't overly muscular; Aedan wasn't so into that. Of course, he'd love Matt however he wanted to have his body. But like this, built but not too bulky, he was absolutely divine.

Aedan enjoyed feeling Matt roll his hips over Aedan's while he ran his hands over Matt's chest. Aedan bit his lip and looked up through his eyelashes.

Today had felt like it was going to overwhelm him completely earlier. Like the blackness might swallow him whole. He hadn't realised how much his low mood had been creeping up on him these past few weeks, gradually getting worse and worse.

But now, thanks to Matt, it felt like the dam had burst and he was all right. Now he was ready to soar again, to start living again, for real.

Matt attacked Aedan's jeans, flicking open the button and drawing down the zip. It wasn't long before he freed Aedan's cock so he could stroke it. Aedan gasped against Matt's mouth. He wanted to be completely naked under Matt, to surrender to him. So he squirmed his way out of the skinny jeans and briefs, then Matt helped yank them down and off his legs.

Matt was easier to strip out of his joggers, the elastic waist slipping easily over his hips to allow him to kick the sweatpants free, leaving them both naked.

"Come here," Aedan said.

He was lying on his back, looking up at Matt as he followed Aedan's instruction and crawled up his body, offering his own cock up for Aedan to lick and suck. Matt gripped the headboard and hovered above, moaning as Aedan swallowed his head and fondled his heavy balls.

"Yes, babe," Matt whispered. Aedan loved it when he used his own favourite moniker.

Aedan released him with a pop. "Do you want to come like this?"

Matt shook his head. "Can we fuck?" he asked. He moved back down to kiss Aedan's mouth and grip the cheek of his arse. Aedan shivered.

Sometimes, he liked to play and put on a show for Matt. They would often switch up positions depending on who felt like what. Aedan felt confident and secure to try anything with Matt. But there were times he just needed to be claimed.

This was one of those times.

Matt loomed over him, a possessive look in his eyes as he gripped the back of Aedan's head to kiss him tenderly.

"Yes," Aedan told him. "I want you inside me, please."

Matt nodded, kissing him again, biting his lip and thrusting with his tongue. He was desperate for Aedan, and that turned Aedan on even more.

Aedan lay back and watched as Matt reached over to the nightstand for the lube. They hadn't needed to bother with condoms for years. Aedan loved the sensation of nothing at all between them, like they melded into one when they made love.

He brushed his hands up and down Matt's arms as he squeezed the silky gel onto his fingers. Already he was relaxing his body, preparing to let Matt in. Matt smiled down as he began to stroke Aedan's hole, pressing his middle finger inside like he had so many times before.

"You look so beautiful," he said, kissing Aedan's lips gently.

Aedan grinned and flicked his eyebrows. "Good enough to eat?"

Matt snorted, but he still began kissing his way down Aedan's chest. Despite his eagerness to feel Matt's hard cock up his arse, Aedan wouldn't say no to a quick bit of foreplay, especially if it loosened him up a bit.

Matt continued trailing kisses down his stomach, his finger still pulsing in Aedan's hole. Aedan groaned and gripped the sheets as Matt licked his cock, sucking on the tip briefly before carrying on to kiss and nuzzle his balls.

"Yes, yes," Aedan gasped.

Matt slid his finger free as he licked along Aedan's perineum. They used flavoured lubes, and Aedan happened to know this one was a festive orange and spiced cinnamon because it was one of the early Christmas purchases he *had* made. Matt obviously approved; he hummed as he began to lick it from Aedan's loosening hole.

"Oh my god, yes, like that," Aedan cried.

He was tempted to wank himself off, but he wanted to wait, to make the release even better when it finally came. Instead he writhed on the bed as Matt ate him out, pinning his hips down so he wouldn't wriggle as much.

Aedan could have taken it for hours. But he needed Matt more than ever now. So after a few minutes he reluctantly ran his fingers through Matt's hair.

"Want you," he begged. "Now. It's okay."

Matt wiped his mouth and raised his eyebrows. Aedan nodded. He'd do the rest of the work as Matt slid inside him.

Aedan bent his legs up so his knees were almost at his shoulders, his heels by his hips. He moaned as Matt cared for him, pressing two fingers inside.

"Yes, oh, babe, yes."

He reached down to stroke Matt's dick, making it fully erect as it dripped a little precum. Aedan yearned for it to fill him. He wanted to feel Matt with every inch of his body.

Aedan found the lube and slicked Matt's cock up so it was gleaming in the ethereal fairy lights. Matt smiled and kissed Aedan passionately. He tasted of orange and cinnamon. Matt removed his fingers then lined himself up and nudging his way inside. Aedan gasped at the intrusion, but it was familiar and welcome. More pleasure than discomfort.

"Yes, babe, just like that," Aedan mumbled between kisses. "Does it feel good?"

Matt was panting. "So good," he stuttered. "God, you're gorgeous. So perfect. All mine."

Aedan smirked and kissed him with glee, both from happiness and the lingering wine in his veins. They both did like to talk nonsense while they were fucking sometimes. But he loved it. It was raw and uninhibited and so very honest.

"All yours," he agreed as Matt pushed his way in further. Half the time, it took too long to prepare for full anal. When they were horny and happy and had work the next day, blow jobs and frotting did just fine. But, Christ. It was so worth it when they took the time to go the whole distance.

There wasn't much talking as Aedan focused on relaxing, opening up and letting Matt in. They hovered with their mouths millimetres apart, gasping in each other's pants and grunts. They both had their fingers gripped into the flesh of the other's back. Aedan's cock thrummed as it bumped against Matt's belly.

When Matt bottomed out they both uttered cries into the quiet flat. Their space. There was no holding back between these walls.

It didn't take Aedan long to grow accustomed to Matt's intrusion. He rolled his hips, thrusting his arse upwards, urging Matt to find his prostate and set him alight with pleasure. They were kissing again, undulating until Matt's cock brushed that magic bundle of nerves and Aedan wailed.

Matt was trembling all over. "That's it, sweetheart," he stammered.

"Yes, yes," said Aedan, urging him on.

They thrust together, the sounds of their cries of ecstasy and slapping of skin bouncing off the walls. Aedan felt wholly complete.

Sometimes he begged to slow it down at this point, make the pleasure last. Not tonight. Tonight, he chased his release.

He cradled Matt's face with one hand, digging his fingers into his flank with the other. They looked into each other's eyes as Aedan felt his climax build.

"Don't stop."

Matt shook his head.

They moved as one, their urgency building to an unavoidable conclusion. Matt took one of his hands and grabbed Aedan's cock.

A couple of tugs was all it took.

Stars exploded behind Aedan's eyelids as his entire body

convulsed with the force of his orgasm. Matt plunged into his body again and again, until his back snapped upwards and he quivered as he peaked to perfection.

Aedan clung to his beautiful lover as his senses gradually returned to him. They gulped down breaths, slowly coming back to the world.

Matt kissed him softly. "That was amazing," he said sleepily. Aedan nodded. His whole body felt like jelly.

"I love you," he said, caressing Matt's jaw and his lips.

Matt kissed him again. "I love you too, Aedan."

It was rare that they ever actually called each other by their given names. It made the moments they did special. Aedan already felt like they were sharing something particularly poignant after the day he'd had, but that sealed it.

Matt slipped out of him gently, cleaning the cum from their bodies with a couple of tissues. They were covered in a sheen of perspiration, their hair plastered to their heads and sweet-smelling lube smeared numerous places. But Aedan didn't care. He was sore in all the right ways and felt a contentment deep in his heart. He pulled Matt back to him.

They laid side by side, gazing sleepily at each other in the faint illumination from the fairy lights. It was all Aedan needed though to look into Matt's eyes as exhaustion crept through his bones.

He didn't need to tell Matt that he loved him again. He already knew.

Finally, Aedan was able to let go of all the troubles that had been plaguing him, allowing them to melt away. He shuffled over to rest his head on Matt's chest, and they held hands in the near-darkness as sleep eventually took them.

Aedan's final thought was that he couldn't wait for Christmas in the morning.

6

ALL I WANT FOR CHRISTMAS IS YOU

A SHARP BANGING AT THE DOOR ROUSED AEDAN BACK INTO consciousness several hours later. It was still dark outside, but it wasn't long before his alarm was due to go off. They may not have been driving to Matt's mum's for a few more hours, but they wanted to enjoy their morning together without rushing.

Matt was dead to the world, so Aedan untangled himself and quickly pulled on his dressing gown as the knocking came again. It was just before seven in the morning.

He hastily made sure he was decent before yanking open the door. He would hate to accidentally flash a neighbour on Christmas morning.

"Merry Christmas," he whispered. He was aware that if there was anyone else left in the nearby flats they might well be sleeping.

The woman in the hall smiled tiredly back at him. She had a sound asleep toddler in one arm and a large suitcase handle gripped in the other hand. The guy behind her wrestled with several sturdy carrier bags filled with wrapped presents and a grumbling little boy of about five.

"Oh thank goodness," said the woman, genuine relief spreading across her face. "I would have felt awful not catching you before we left." She thrust a squishy parcel into his hands, the brown paper wrapped around it well crumpled. "I took this in for you yesterday and worried it was a Christmas present."

Aedan's eyes widened as they took in the international postmark and then filled with tears. "It's for my boyfriend," he said, his voice hoarse. "Thank you. Really, thank you."

The adults smiled and nodded as they made their way towards the stairs. "Have a wonderful Christmas," the guy said.

"You too," Aedan replied.

He closed the door. A mildly hysterical giggle escaped his lips, then he hurried back into the bedroom. He couldn't believe his luck.

"Matt," he hissed, kissing his boyfriend's cheeks and forehead. "Wake up, it's Christmas! And guess what? Matt. *Matt?*"

He watched as Matt stirred and rubbed his eyes, all adorable and rumpled. A smile slowly spread across his face. "Merry Christmas, darling," he said, fumbling clumsily to reach for Aedan's arm.

Aedan gave him another chaste kiss on his nose, then placed the long-awaited package on the nightstand by the bed. He knew Matt well enough now to know this could only be fixed with coffee.

Aedan hummed to himself as he clattered around in the kitchen, allowing the smell of the brew and his slightly over the top rummaging to wake up his boyfriend fully.

That old familiar Christmas giddiness thrummed through his veins for the first time all year.

He found a box of mince pies in the cupboard and returned to the bedroom with them and two mugs of steaming hot coffee. "Hey, babe," he said as he was greeted with Matt's sleepy smile.

"Hey," was his reply as he stretched and eased his way up into a sitting position. "Merry Christmas."

Aedan bounded over to him, carefully not to spill their drinks but too excited to restrain himself. "Your present came," he blurted out, useless to keep a surprise like this. "It's stupid, and you'll probably think I'm an idiot. But it came and-"

Matt pulled him by his robe down for a kiss. "I don't think it's stupid in the slightest."

Aedan arched an eyebrow. "You have no idea what it is yet."

"So?" said Matt, seizing his coffee eagerly and taking a sip. "I already know it's awesome."

Aedan laughed. "You just want to open it right now."

Matt nodded. "Oh hell yeah." He laughed, his eyes sparkling.

Aedan's heart fluttered. He meant it, it was a stupid present. But he was so sure Matt would appreciate it. He hoped it was worth all the fuss.

He picked up the package but held onto it as he slipped back under the covers with his own coffee. "You don't mind it in its crappy original wrapping?" he asked with a scoff.

Matt shook his head and made grabby hands.

Aedan sighed and hoped his gamble would pay off. If not, there was still his steadfast presents waiting under the tree.

Matt made short work of the packaging, despite the copious amounts of tape wrapped around the thing. Then he had the distributor's own plastic bag to tear through, but he was laughing, so Aedan knew he didn't mind. Aedan, on the other hand, was chewing his thumbnail.

It was obvious as soon as Matt got through the wrapping

that it was a jumper. But when he shook it out, that was when he gasped, joy lighting up his face.

"It's musical, too," said Aedan. He leaned forwards and groped for the button he knew should be there waiting for him.

Sure enough, when he found the right pressure point, tinny music suddenly blared into the tranquillity of their flat.

"Make my wish come trueeeee!" the voice sang. *"All I want for Christmaaas – is YOU!"*

The ugly jumper had the title lyrics knitted into the front to match. Because it *was* true.

"All I want for Christmas is you," he said to Matt.

Matt laughed, his eyes glassy as he stared at the ghastly creation. "I love it," he said. "It's perfect. I'm going to wear it all week." Then he looked at Aedan. "But mine's frighteningly similar. Do you want it now?"

Aedan chuckled, seriously hoping he hadn't got a hideous jumper as well. He liked kitsch. Fugly was Matt's M.O. But he nodded eagerly all the same.

Matt hugged his jumper with obvious affection, making Aedan's heart sing. He surged forwards and kissed Aedan on the lips. "You have to close your eyes for a sec."

Aedan huffed, not sure why there was a need for subterfuge. They'd wrapped their presents last night. But he did as he was told, dutifully closing his eyes.

Matt kissed his cheek again, then Aedan felt him leave the bed and heard him pull his own dressing gown from the back of their bedroom door and rustle into it. There were a few seconds of silence where he presumably went to go retrieve his present. Come to think of it though, Aedan didn't remember seeing a gift addressed to him under the tree last night.

"Okay," said Matt. His voice sounded a bit strange. "You can open your eyes now."

Grinning, Aedan complied.

Then his heart all but stopped.

Matt was by the side of the bed. On one knee.

Aedan squawked in the most undignified manner as he slapped his hands over his mouth, tears springing immediately into his eyes.

Matt was trembling from head to toe. But his hands were steady as they held up the ring box towards Aedan.

"I love you so much," Matt managed to croak. He cleared his throat and grinned sheepishly. "Aedan, will you marry me?"

Aedan almost fell off the bed in his haste to throw his arms around Matt's neck. This couldn't be happening. He couldn't possibly be this lucky, this blessed.

"*Babe!*" he shrieked, shaking just as badly as Matt had been. "Oh my god, babe. Oh my god, *oh my GOD! YES!*"

Matt was laughing as he pulled him to the carpet, tangling them both together. "Oh thank god, I was going crazy holding that in."

"You proposed," said Aedan, hardly daring to believe it. Tears streamed down his face, the happy kind though this time. "You really want to spend the rest of your life with me?"

Matt took a deep breath and maneuvered them so they were both sat on the floor. He held the ring box in one hand and cupped Aedan's cheek with the other. "Yes," he said. "Please don't ever doubt it."

Aedan wiped his face and bounced on his heels. "Can I see the ring?" he begged, unashamedly.

Matt laughed, a throaty sound where he dropped his head back. His relief was palpable. He first leaned over to touch his lips to Aedan's; a kiss filled with so many promises. Then he offered up the box. "Just something to add a little sparkle to the season," he said, in a turn of phrase that sounded an awful lot like Aunt Eileen's life-long mantra.

It was stunning. Aedan couldn't have picked better himself.

It was a solid silver coloured band, although when he picked it up he suspected the metal was platinum. Across the band in a diagonal were three fat diamonds, flanked by two fine stripes of very small and delicate looking diamonds. It fit perfectly on Aedan's finger.

He choked back a sob as he admired it, then dragged Matt back into another hug. "This is the best gift you could ever…I'm so…"

He couldn't seem to finish a thought.

Matt didn't need him to. He kissed his lips and looked into his eyes. Aedan's horrendous but fabulous Christmas jumper had fallen to the floor alongside them, and Matt picked it up to show Aedan the inscription.

"All I want for Christmas is you," he said with a grin.

"All I want *forever*," Aedan amended, "is you."

THANK YOU

Thank You

Dear Reader,

Out of all the many books out there, you chose this one to read. Thank you. It means so much to share my tales of love, drama and happy-ever-afters with you all.

If you enjoyed reading Matt and Aedan's story, I would very much appreciate it if you would like to share your experience with others online. Reviews, recommendations, fan works and general love is the best way for me to reach new readers.

If you'd like to meet with more of my fans, why not join our Facebook group? Helen Juliet Books. We're very friendly! You can also subscribe to my newsletter via www.helenjuliet.com for news and extra freebie scenes from all my books!

Lots of love,

Helen

ACKNOWLEDGMENTS

Thank you to my mum for keeping me sane through this one. It was surprisingly tricky for such a tiny thing. Thanks also to my brother for his great work.

Credit and kudos to Meg Cooper for the editing and Natasha Snow for the cover.

Love and thanks to my husband and kitties for bringing the glitter and sparkle in their own unique ways.

ABOUT THE AUTHOR

Helen Juliet is a contemporary MM romance author living in London with her husband and two balls of fluff that occasionally pretend to be cats. She began writing at an early age, later honing her craft online in the world of fanfiction on sites like Wattpad. Fifteen years and over a million words later, she sought out original MM novels to read. She never thought she would be any good at romance, but once she turned her hand to it she discovered she in fact adored it. By the end of 2016 she had written her first book of her own, and in 2017 she fulfilled her lifelong dream of becoming a fulltime author.

Glitter on the Garland is Helen's first published work. She also writes contemporary American MM romance as HJ Welch.

You can contact Helen Juliet via social media:
Newsletter – Subscribe at www.helenjuliet.com for news and FREEBIES!
Website – www.helenjuliet.com
Email – helenjulietauthor@gmail.com
Twitter – @helenjwrites
Instagram – @helenjwrites
Tumblr – @helenjwrites

Facebook Page – @HelenJulietAuthor
Facebook Group – Helen Juliet Books

A Ballad of Confetti, Cake and Catastrophes

Nicholas Herald's only job was to book the music for his sister's wedding. So when the big day is only a week away and the job isn't done, his options are running out fast. In the end he throws down his cash on a guitarist with nimble fingers and arresting eyes.

Fynn Dumashie is more than happy to spend time with Nicholas as they feverishly plan the wedding's music together. But the closer they get to the event, the more Nicholas seems to want something more... If only he could stop fighting himself to ask for it.

With last minute cancellations, wayward family members, and a cat with a serious vendetta against happiness, they'll be lucky if they make it to the wedding in one piece. Can Nicholas overcome his own fears to accept who he really is before he and Fynn part ways for the last time?

A Ballad of Confetti, Cake and Catastrophes is a steamy, standalone gay romance novel with a HEA and no cliffhanger.